4/27/19.

To Valentina
God bless you abundantly.
Caroleane Rice

THE LADYBUG AND THE BULLY FROG

THE LADYBUG AND THE BULLY FROG

by

Caroleann Rice

XULON PRESS

Xulon Press
2301 Lucien Way #415
Maitland, FL 32751
407.339.4217
www.xulonpress.com

© 2018 By Caroleann Rice, Illustrations by Charles Berton

Unless otherwise indicated, Scripture quotations taken from Scripture quotations taken from the King James Version (KJV)–*public domain*.

Printed in the United States of America.
Edited by Xulon Press.

ISBN-13: 9781545634998

Visit Caroleann Rice at:
www.MrsLadyBug.com
Email: CaroleannRice@aol.com

Charles Berton can be found at:
www.CharlesBerton.com

I give thanks and honor to the Mighty Wondrous Voice of Love for the characters and words written in this book.

Thank you, Kevin, for your encouragement and your skill in helping me to create this book, love you much.

Thank you, Colleen, for your encouragement as well and helping with many daily responsibilities so I could devote time to writing. Love you too, so much.

Thank you, Charles, for being such a gifted illustrator. You, with your wonderful artistry, are a blessing from God.

To the Women of the Well, my spiritual sisters, your prayers and love are heartfelt. Thank you all. I especially want to say thank you to Susan for her support and love in helping me to bring these characters and story about. She traveled with me to the Amish Country in Pennsylvania where I was blessed to hear part of the title of this book "The Bully Frog" and his name "Milton." The Mighty Wondrous Voice of Love blessed me with you, love you dear friend.

And finally to Xulon Press I say thank you, thank you, for all your help and expertise.

You are all a gift in my life, and for this I am grateful. Give thanks to the Lord for He is good* – always! Thank you, Lord, for always being so good and merciful!

* Psalm 107:1, paraphrased from the King James -
"Oh give thanks to the Lord for He is good.
His mercy endures forever."

As the story opens we find Clover the Rabbit asking Lance the Snake:

"Did you hear what happened to Milton the Frog? Did you hear what our friends are saying? Skeeter the Mosquito and Mugsy the Bee had given a party and invited all they knew, the wasps and hornets and a few more mosquitoes too. Oh boy! Have you heard? They caused a big problem when they didn't ask Milton the Frog to join in the fun. Milton became sad and would talk to no one."

"Poor Milton kept his sadness inside and was mean to all who would come to be with him at the pond, right down the stream from where we played."

"It wasn't right! It wasn't fair! To keep Milton the Frog away from joining in the fun at the party that day!"

Everyone was buzzing and chattering away, talking about Milton in an unfriendly way.

"You would be hurt too if someone you knew was making fun of you. And now calling you a 'Bully'? What a name to live up to!" said Petunia and Pansy the Bumblebee twins who are ever so much fun to be with. They giggle and laugh and love to have all their friends come and join in the fun down at the pond.

Petunia and Pansy the Bumble bee twins were worried, and so was the village of friends. "What can we do to help Milton to be happy again?"

"I know," said Clover the Rabbit. "I'll just hop over to Ladybug Dot's house and she'll talk to Solomon the very wise Snail!"

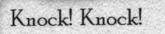

Knock! Knock!

"Can you open up to me? It's Clover. I've come to have a cup of tea, and talk about how to help a friend in need."

Sooo! Ladybug Dot opened the door and welcomed her in.

"Please," said Clover. "We need to get help quick! Milton the Frog is a bully now!"

"So I have heard," said Mrs. Ladybug. "Even my children can't play down at the pond. It seems no one is welcomed by Milton the Frog. Sit down, relax, enjoy a cup of tea. The Mighty Wondrous Voice of Love will send wise Solomon to me. For He knows everything. Solomon the Snail told me to just go inside my room and ask the Mighty Wondrous Voice of Love to come and help. I know Solomon the Snail would hear it too, so let's go visit Solomon the Snail who is ever so wise, and ask him what to do."

After Clover the Rabbit and Dot the Ladybug finished their tea, they travelled down the road to where Solomon the Snail would be. As they went on their way Clover the Rabbit hopped on ahead, and the Ladybug Dot, flying over the trees, said, "I see him. His chimney is smoking. He's inside his house. We'll knock on the door. He'll be happy to see us and be glad that we came."

Knock! Knock!

"Solomon, it's Clover the Rabbit and Mrs. Ladybug. We have come here to seek your advice."

As the door began to creak open, there Solomon appeared. "Good day to you my dear sweet friends. Oh, but you both look so troubled. You both look so sad. How can I help you to be happy again?"

"Oh Solomon," said Clover. "Oh Solomon," said Dot, both at the same time.

"One at a time," said Solomon. "I know you're in a rush to get your problem solved but when you're both chattering at the same time it's not easy to hear and make sense. Let's be quiet a moment, and then, one at a time, let's talk about what's going on." After a quick pause, Solomon looked at his friend the rabbit.

"It's Milton the Frog," said Clover. "He decided to be a Bully Frog and he has taken over the pond."

"The village of friends can't enjoy meeting and playing there," said Dot. "We can't change him, and everyone is afraid. They won't go down to see him because he's angry and sad. You know it to be true. That is why he chases us all away. Oh, what are we to do?"

Solomon, being so very wise, said, "Dot, we have been friends for a while. What would the Mighty Wondrous Voice of Love tell us to do? Think LOVE. Love heals all things. Love heals the wounds. It's love that Milton needs. I know you're afraid but, Dot, the words to heal Milton will have to come from you."

"But Solomon, can't you go for me? I'm afraid of his angry voice and his unhappy face. He scares me when he wants to chase me away."

"I know," said Solomon the wise snail. "Call on Mighty Wondrous Voice of Love. He will never fail. He will be with you wherever you go. Be strong! Be courageous! So off you go."

Ladybug Dot had no choice but to go, yet she knew that the Mighty Wondrous Voice of Love would be with her too.

She could see Milton as she flew over the trees. Oh! There he is! There is Milton, taking over the pond, and he won't let anyone in, she said to herself. He was lying in the pond with one leg over his knee, his arms behind his head. "I think I'll fly and land on his big toe," she softy said, "so I can keep away from his head."

As Dot the Ladybug flew down from the trees, she saw Mugsy the Bee and Skeeter the Mosquito hiding and laughing, saying to themselves, "Who does she think she is? She's so small, and all by herself. All Milton has to do is holler and yell and she'll faint. She'll be all by herself."

"Ha! Ha! Ha!" they laughed, "I can't wait to see what happens to her," said Mugsy to Skeeter. "Some silly ladybug she'll soon be."

As they watched from the bushes, Mrs. Ladybug, whose friends call her Dot, flew down and landed right on the spot, on Milton's big toe.

Oh boy, was he surprised! Shocked even. "Oh, ho!" he exclaimed. Caught by surprise, he stared at her. She stared at him.

"Well! What brings you to see me and who is going to talk first, you or me? You have heard what I'm going to do, so I'll give you one last chance to fly away quick because I am much bigger than you!"

"I'm not going anywhere. I came because I have a message for you, and also to ask a question or two. How do you feel, Milton, now that you have chased everyone away? What you did was selfish and it has now turned on you. You're all alone, Milton, with no one to care about you. That makes you unhappy and keeps you from being friendly.

"Milton, didn't you sing your song at night? You have stopped because you have no love. While all was quiet and all was still we could hear you sing your song. We need to hear a new song, Milton. Call again to your friends to come to the pond and play, and they will come the very next day."

Then Dot spoke to Milton about the Mighty Wondrous Voice of Love.

After Ladybug Dot spoke to Milton about the Mighty Wondrous Voice of Love, Mugsy the Bee and Skeeter the Mosquito flew off in joy and glee. They couldn't believe what they saw with their own eyes and heard with their own ears. "The whole countryside of friends needs to hear the news! Just maybe we have hope of coming together again and we would be forgiven too." So off they flew with the good news.

But Ladybug Dot continued to stay with Milton, and talked, and talked and talked some more. She told him about the Mighty Wondrous Voice of Love, and how wonderful it is to hear Love say, "I have waited sooooo long to love you today."

Milton finally asked, "Can I ask the Mighty Wondrous Voice of Love if He can help me?"

"Sure He can," said Ladybug Dot. "The Voice of Love has been waiting for you. Just say, 'Mighty Wondrous Voice of Love, will you hear me now?' Tell Him how you have been hurting and angry because no one wanted to be with you and the Mighty Wondrous Voice of Love will hear you, Milton."

Milton stared at the ladybug as he thought and thought and thought some more.

"But before I go," said Ladybug Dot, "I want to invite you to come to my home on Rose Bush Lane and I will make you your favorite lily cream pie so you can be with the children and me."

"You invite me? The one whom nobody likes? You invite me? You invite Milton 'the Bully Frog' as I am now called? Hip Hip Hurray! And Yikes! I'll do it! Now, Ladybug Dot, you hurry off! Fly away, fly away home," said Milton. "I'll come later around three o'clock and I promise to tell you how I spoke to the Mighty Wondrous Voice of Love and what He had to say. Oh boy! I can hardly wait to have my favorite pie."

After Ladybug Dot flew away, Milton was all alone. He sat up in the pond, looked up at the sky and called on the Mighty Wondrous Voice of Love.

"Oh Mighty Wondrous Voice of Love, can You help me? I'm not sure if You are here but I am asking just the same," said Milton. And he continued to ask, "I don't know how and this is the best I can do. You know what is in my heart. I'm sad and I'm angry too. Please I need an answer from You. Sometimes I can't help it but I think the only one that can help me now is You. I know this much, all right – if You want me to change then You need to answer me quick because I miss all my friends especially my friend the snake called Lance."

Milton became very still...

And then...

All of a sudden he broke out in a smile, and for a while he began to shout, "Oh boy! Oh joy! I heard Mighty Wondrous Voice of Love! I heard the Voice of Love tell me what I am to do! I'm happy and joyful thanks to Ladybug Dot! The time is now. I need to leave the pond and be on my way. I can't be late to Ladybug Dot's house. Wait till she hears what I have to say!"

So as the story goes, Milton left the pond to go to Rose Bush Lane. When he arrived he knocked at the door. Dot the Ladybug opened the door and all her children hid behind her in fear. But Milton told them, "You don't have to be afraid of me anymore because I'm so happy to be here."

"May I hug him, Mom?" "Can I hug him too?" said one, and then another of the ladybug children. "Please, Mom, he's changed."

"Yes you may," said Ladybug Dot. "I can see that too! Let's have some of Milton's favorite pie and hear what he has to say, for he spoke to the Mighty Wondrous Voice of Love today."

They all had a piece of Milton's favorite pie, and when they finished the ladybug children couldn't wait to hear what Milton had to say.

"Come on Milton," said one child. "Yeah come on," said another.

"Children be patient and wait," said Ladybug Dot. "He'll tell us when you calm down. Remember, you need to hear this too."

So Milton began to tell them what the Mighty Wondrous Voice of Love had to say. "He told me, 'Love your neighbor as yourself and I love you too. Ask your friends to forgive you and say, "Once again can we play, down by the pond, and be silly and happy just the way that we used to be?" But most of all, sing your night song. Sing a new song, Milton, and tell all your friends about Me. Invite them to come out at night and sing along with you.'"

Milton continued, "The Voice of Love told me how I was forgiven and much-loved too. I can do this, Ladybug Dot. Thank you, thank you, I'm happy again. If it wasn't for you I would have no friends. You have courage. Your children are blessed to have you."

"I need to go soon and change up my ways, and show everyone I'm different this day. Friends again, friends again! Hip Hip Hurray!"

So Milton thanked Ladybug Dot. The children asked their mom, "Can we go with Milton, Mom?" All the children did ask. "We want to hear Milton sing his new song. Oh please. We'll sit on the grass and we'll sing too."

"All right, children. I'll take you. We'll fly over the pond and hear Milton sing."

We come to the close of this story of how the Mighty Wondrous Voice of Love changed Milton's frown into a smile. Come to think of it, a smile is catchy. It's better than a frown. Why don't you try it today – Smile the Milton Frog way!